Ghost Rescue

AND THE
SPACE GHOST

Ghost Rescue

AND THE SPACE GHOST

WRITTEN BY
Andrew Murray

ILLUSTRATED BY
Sarah Horne

ORCHARD BOOKS

ORCHARD BOOKS

338 Euston Road, London NW1 3BH

Orchard Books Australia

Level 17/207 Kent Street, Sydney, NSW 2000

First published in hardback in Great Britain in 2009 by Orchard Books

First published in paperback in 2010

ISBN 978 1 84616 357 9 (hardback)

ISBN 978 1 84616 366 1 (paperback)

Text © Andrew Murray 2009

Illustrations © Sarah Horne 2009

A CIP catalogue record for this book is available from the British Library.

1 3 5 7 9 10 8 6 4 2 (hardback)

3 5 7 9 10 8 6 4 2 (paperback)

Printed in Great Britain

Orchard Books is a division of Hachette Children's Books,

an Hachette UK company.

www.hachette.co.uk

Thud! A rocket landed in Charlie's back garden. Charlie should have been asleep, but he had been looking at the stars, wondering whether there were any aliens up there.

Now he rushed outside, with the Ghost Rescue ghosts following close behind. There was Lord and Lady Fairfax, their daughter Florence, Zanzibar the dog and Rio the parrot.

"Who on earth is firing rockets?"
said Lord Fairfax.

"It's not the fourth of July,"
said Charlie.

"And it's not the fifth of November,"
added Florence.

"Careful, Charlie," warned Lady Fairfax. "You should never approach a rocket, in case it explodes."

"Don't worry, Lady F," smiled Charlie. "I don't think this one is going to—"

BANG!

They all ducked, then looked up. The rocket hadn't exploded. Instead, a side panel had blown away, and a screen had popped out. Charlie and Ghost Rescue crept closer. The screen was showing an image of a wheat field with a great dome in the background. And in the field was a kind of circular machine, lying smoking and crumpled in a crater.

"That looks like some sort of vehicle," said Lady F.

"A flying vehicle, perhaps?" added her husband.

"A flying…plate?" suggested Florence.

"A flying saucer!" said Charlie. "And I know where that place is. It's the Starfunkel Observatory, not far from here. And this must be the distress rocket the flying saucer fired. Come on, my friends – Ghost Rescue is *go!*"

In no time at all, Ghost Rescue were racing along the starlit roads in their Ghostmobile, an old pizza delivery van.

Soon the Ghostmobile was driving slowly through the wheat field near the observatory. As always, Charlie was slumped down below the windscreen so he could reach the pedals, and the ghosts told him where to go. But this time the Fairfaxes couldn't see anything either, except a sea of wheat. Florence decided to float up above the Ghostmobile to get a better view. It was a good thing she did.

"*STOP!*" she yelled. "Charlie, stop!"

Suddenly the sea of wheat parted. The van stopped, just centimetres from the crater.

They saw the smoke first, then the crater, then the wreck of the flying saucer. An alien's body sat in the pilot's seat.

"Is he dead?" asked Florence.

Charlie bent over him, and sighed. "Dead as a dodo. I wonder what happens to aliens when they die? Do they become—"

"*Ptup mbump znabdookoo?*"

Everyone jumped in surprise. Zanzibar growled and Rio squawked.

Ghost Rescue took a look at the ghost they were rescuing. It had four ears, three eyes, two noses and one mouth, which opened and said:

"*Proo?*"

"Um," said Charlie, not sure how to begin. "Hello? We mean you no harm."

"*Bnib bnob?*" said the alien ghost.

"I don't think he speaks English," said Lord Fairfax.

"How about French?" said Florence.

"I think he comes from a bit further away than France, dear," smiled her mother.

"Zbuppa duppa!"

The alien ghost drifted over to his body, and gestured at his spacesuit. He pointed at the face mask, pointed at his own mouth, then pointed at Charlie's mouth.

"He's trying to tell us something," said
Lady F.

"Is he hungry?" suggested Florence.

"Ghosts don't need food, dear," said
her mother.

"How do you know what *space* ghosts
need?" said Florence crossly.

"Aha!" said Charlie. "I think I've got it!" He crawled into the cockpit and examined the space suit, looking for an opening. He found it – a zip ran all the way up the back of the suit.

Carefully, Charlie started to undo the zip. He looked at the alien ghost. "Am I doing the right thing?"

"*Bna bna bna!*"

Charlie struggled to get the alien's body out of his suit. When the last boot was off, he settled the body back in the seat, and gently closed all three of its eyes. Then Charlie took a closer look at the face mask. He saw that there was a dial on the front, marked with strange alien symbols.

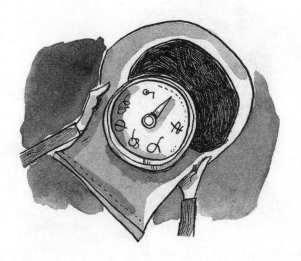

Charlie put the mask over his head, and said, "Hello?"

Charlie's voice came out unchanged.

"It doesn't do anything," said Lady F.

"Try turning the dial," said Lord F.

Charlie did, and tried speaking again. This time his "hello" became "*K-K-K-!-§-Ø-?-™-X-X-X??*"

The alien ghost covered his ears, and shook his head.

"Wrong language, I suppose," said Charlie. He turned the dial again.

"*Ptup mbump znabdookoo?*"

The alien ghost laughed and clapped his hands with excitement. Then he pointed at the mask again.

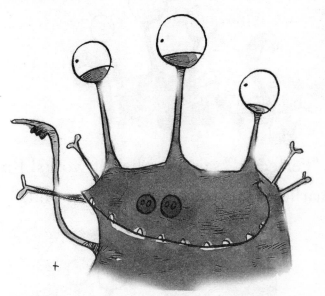

Charlie hadn't noticed the four earpieces hanging off the sides. He climbed into the suit properly this time, zipping it up over his head, fitting the mask over his face and sticking two of the earpieces in his ears. The suit was hot, and smelled like tuna fish and shampoo.

"Hello!" said the alien ghost. "Can you hear me now?"

"Perfectly!" said Charlie. "It works! I'm Charlie Cormac. Pleased to meet you."

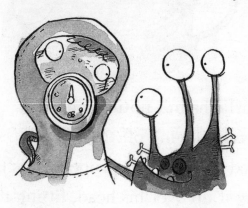

"And I am Zibron Ziboo, from the planet Loopaper. Greetings from all my people!"

"Sorry," said Charlie, "Did you say *Loopaper?*"

"Yes," said Zibron. "Why, have you heard of it?"

"I…er…oh, never mind," grinned Charlie. "So, Zibron, how can Ghost Rescue help?"

"I need to send an SOS to my people," said Zibron. "But my radio transmitter broke in the crash. Is there another powerful radio transmitter round here?"

"A powerful radio transmitter?" said Charlie. "Goodness, I don't know…"

Charlie found the Earthling setting on the translator dial, and told the Fairfaxes what Zibron had said. They all thought long and hard.

"Hmm," pondered Florence. "A radio transmitter..."

"...Strong enough to send a message into space," added Lord F.

"What kind of place would have such a thing?" asked Lady F.

Then they looked at each other, and then up at the dome of the Starfunkel Observatory. Beside the telescope, glinting in the early morning sun, was a tall radio aerial.

"*Of course!*"

Zibron's ghost was tied to his ship, so he told Charlie what to say in the SOS. Then Charlie crept into the observatory.

There was nobody around. Charlie tiptoed over to the radio room and turned on the microphone at the desk.

Then Charlie recited the message Zibron had given him – an SOS to the people of Loopaper. The translator mask turned his words into Loopaperite:

"*Zevnopoo! Zevnopoo! Illa Zibron Ziboo, fnubti oigog proo! Illa Zibron Ziboo, fnubti oigog proo...*"

Far out in space, on the planet Loopaper, a radio station operator picked up the signal.

"Sir, sir, it's Zibron Ziboo! He's crashed on Earth, and he needs help!"

And a rescue party set off for Earth, not realising that Zibron was a ghost.

Zibron looked into the sky. "Charlie must have sent the SOS by now," he smiled. "Rescue is on its way. Nothing to worry about now!"

Back in the radio room, Charlie smiled. "Nothing to worry about now!" he said, and with a big sigh of relief he leaned his elbow on the desk...

...on a button...

...marked, WARNING: TELESCOPE RELEASE.

FFFSSSSHHH... With a heavy, oily noise, the telescope slipped free, and swung down, and...

CRACK!

Charlie scarcely had time to look up before the telescope smashed into his face. Everything went black...

...and Charlie woke up to find the ghosts anxiously leaning over him.

"He's coming round! He's going to be all right!"

"Charlie? Can you hear me? Charlie, how do you feel?" said Florence.

Charlie's head felt like someone had dragged his brain out of his ear with hooks, and shoved it back in again with spikes. Through the pain, he struggled to say, "Yes, I'm OK" – but no sound came out of the translator. He twiddled the translator dial, and tried again, but still the ghosts couldn't hear a word.

Charlie felt all over the mask with his hands. It had taken the full force of the blow, and was badly cracked and dented. Clearly the translator was as dead as Zibron.

Oh well, no point in wearing this suit any more, thought Charlie, and he reached to undo the zip. He grabbed the end of the zip and pulled. Nothing happened. He tried again. The zip wouldn't budge.

"Oh come *on!*" moaned Charlie.
"Come on, you…stupid…*thing*!"

But it was no use. The impact of the
telescope had jammed the zip as surely
as it had broken the translator.

Charlie broke into a clammy sweat
as he realised he was trapped inside
Zibron's suit.

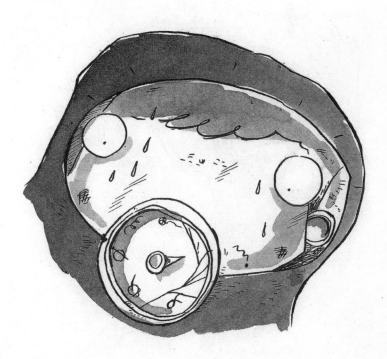

"*Help! Get me out of this thing!*" he cried, but of course the ghosts couldn't hear a word.

"Why isn't Charlie saying anything?" said Lord F. "Charlie, *talk* to us."

Charlie pointed frantically at the translator.

"Is there something wrong with your face, Charlie?" asked Lady F.

Charlie nodded.

"Are you having trouble breathing?" asked Florence.

Charlie shook his head.

"I've got it!" said Lord F. "You're hungry, is that it?"

Charlie shook his head and stamped his foot in frustration.

Then they all realised…

"Of *course!* The translator's broken! And the zip – is that jammed too?"

Charlie breathed a sigh of relief. Some people could be so slow…

They all went back to Zibron's flying saucer. Charlie tried everything: scraping his head along the ground, tugging at the zip with his space-gloves, and even using the toolkit from the Ghostmobile – but it was no use. The zip wouldn't budge.

Meanwhile, the ghosts watched and waited for Zibron's rescuers. Loopaper spaceships can travel faster than the speed of light, and in no time at all Florence exclaimed, "Look!"

In the distance a bright pinpoint of light grew larger and larger. Soon they could see it was a spaceship, following Zibron's SOS message back to its source.

The spaceship paused, seemed to look around, and obviously saw Zibron's flying saucer, because it came zipping over and landed beside them.

It was a larger craft than Zibron's little saucer. When the hatch opened, three aliens emerged, wearing the same suits and masks as Charlie. They marched over to him.

"*Proozoo Zibron, zapwi noobah — ek ek fnarpy garpy robanki itto!*" they said — which meant, "Zibron, good to see you're OK, but we've got to get you out of here before any Earthlings spot us!"

And before anyone had time to think, the aliens were bundling Charlie into their spaceship, attaching a towrope to Zibron's saucer, and *BLASTING* into space.

"*Aaaaaaaaaggggggggggggghhhhhhh!*" howled Charlie, as he went from standstill to the speed of light in a matter of moments. By chance he had his bag containing the Fairfax stone over his shoulder, so the ghosts were riding along too. And behind them came Zibron, dragged by his flying saucer...

In a flash they were in the starry black of space, with planets, comets and asteroids whizzing by. Further and faster they raced, and then one planet grew larger and larger until they could see nothing else. Planet Loopaper!

The ship slowed from the speed of light back to standstill, and landed.

Charlie was trying to get his mind back into one piece as the aliens led him out of the spaceship into a new world...

And what a world it was! The colours!
The plants! The sulphur-yellow sky! The
swarms of giant rainbow-coloured bugs!

And the *people* – the Loopaperites
were a remarkable range of sizes, from
human-sized to giant-sized. One of these
giants was roaming around with some
kind of giant mushroom in his hand,
using it to swat at the bugs – *SWISH!*
SWOOSH!

Charlie was still struggling to undo his zip as the aliens led him away from the ship. The Fairfaxes came with him, but Zibron's ghost was left behind, stuck with his flying saucer.

"*Znoo! Znoo!*" he cried. "Hey! Hey!" But nobody heard him.

The three aliens climbed out of their spacesuits and breathed the Loopaper air.

"Ahh!" said Akki Akkinan in their Loopaper language. "Good fresh sulphur dioxide – you can't beat it!"

"Hey, Zibron," said Zotti Zotto. "Are you going to keep your suit on all day?"

Frantically Charlie pointed at his broken mask and zip.

"What's up with him?" said Pweb.
"He's acting *very* strangely."

"I think his zip might be stuck," said
Akki. "Over here, mate, let me have a
look at it…"

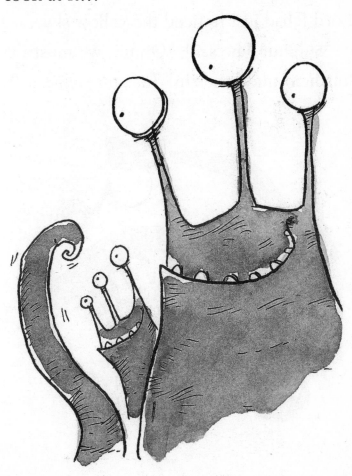

And as the aliens examined Charlie's zip, Lord F was struck by an awful thought. Of course, he hadn't been able to understand a word the Loopaperites said. But, looking around at this strange world, Lord F had just noticed the yellow sky…

"Sulphur!" he said. "Oh no, we mustn't let them undo the zip! *The air's poisonous!*"

What could the Fairfaxes do? How could they make the aliens realise they had the wrong person?

Lord Fairfax looked around. There on a bench was a row of brand-new translator masks. But what good was that? The masks were solid, and he was a ghost.

Just then, the giant with the mushroom
fly-swat came by, swooshing away at
the bugs – and Lord F had an idea. He
concentrated hard, and began to shrink,
and change shape, turning himself into a
particularly large and evil-looking bug.

"Dad!" said Florence. "What are you doing?"

"Oh, Reginald, do be careful!" cried Lady F – but it was too late. Lord F was buzzing around the giant's head.

"*ZBAMMAZATT!*" growled the giant, and the fly-swat *SWISHED* and *SWOOSHED*, missing Lord F by millimetres.

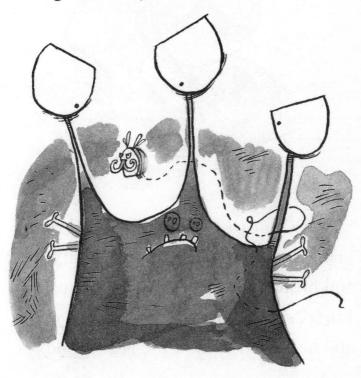

"Your father's gone mad!" snapped Lady F. But her husband knew what he was doing. He buzzed down to the bench, and sat on one of the translator masks.

"*MOOI-BOOI-CHOOI...*" grinned the giant, as he raised the fly-swat high, and brought it down on little Reginald Fairfax. But the Fairfax bug was too quick, and he darted away at the last second.

SMASH!

The bench buckled in the middle, and the translator mask was pulverised into dust.

Lord F resumed his normal shape, and the Fairfaxes stared at the bench. There, where the translator mask had been, pale and smoky, was *the ghost of the translator mask.*

"Of course!" said Lady F. "Everything leaves a ghost when it ceases to be."

"No time to lose!" cried Lord F, as he put on the ghost translator mask.

And not a moment too soon. Akki Akkinan, Zotti Zotto and Pweb were working hard on Charlie's zip, which was starting to loosen…

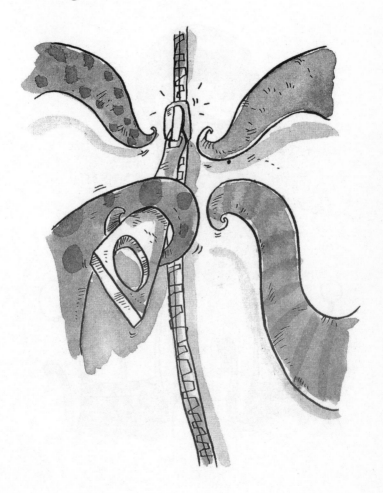

"Stop!" cried Lord F in perfect Loopaperite. "The fellow in that suit is not who you think he is…"

Lord Fairfax explained everything to the aliens, who then did all they could to set things right. First, they made Charlie hold his breath while they tore his broken suit from him and zipped him up in a nice new one.

"Thanks!" panted Charlie in perfect Loopaperite. And, as the rescue ship got ready to return Charlie and Ghost Rescue to Earth, they all said a fond farewell to Zibron.

"You're home, Zibron!" said Charlie.

"Thanks to Ghost Rescue!" called Zibron, and he waved goodbye as the ship zoomed into space.

"Hmm," said Charlie thoughtfully.

"What is it, Charlie?" asked Lord F.

"Oh, I was just thinking," smiled Charlie. "You know we've got our Ghost Rescue site on the *world* wide web... I was just wondering if there's a *universe* wide web we could advertise on..."

And Charlie and the ghosts of Ghost Rescue laughed and laughed at the speed of light!

Ghost Rescue

WRITTEN BY
Andrew Murray

ILLUSTRATED BY
Sarah Horne

All priced at £3.99

The Ghost Rescue books are available from all good bookshops,
or can be ordered direct from the publisher:
Orchard Books, PO BOX 29, Douglas IM99 1BQ
Credit card orders please telephone 01624 836000
or fax 01624 837033 or visit our website: www.orchardbooks.co.uk
or email: bookshop@enterprise.net for details.

To order please quote title, author and ISBN
and your full name and address.
Cheques and postal orders should be made payable to 'Bookpost plc'.
Postage and packing is FREE within the UK
(overseas customers should add £1.00 per book).

Prices and availability are subject to change.